WHEN WE DEAD AWAKEN

A NEW ADAPTATION BY WALTER WYKES

HENRIK IBSEN

Playing w/ relation
btwn art : reality
w/out giving us
any conclusion

Black Box Press
Arlington, TX

ISBN 978-0-6152-1182-4

Second Edition

CONTENTS

In Loving Memory of Carol Joy Beglau (1923-2006)

INTRODUCTION

According to one of Ibsen's contemporaries, *When We Dead Awaken* was written "with such labour and such passionate agitation, so spasmodically and so feverishly, that those around him were almost alarmed . . . He seemed to hear the beating of dark pinions over his head." If the great dramatist did indeed have a premonition of his impending death, this play, subtitled "a dramatic epilogue," may be regarded as a sort of last confession, Ibsen's final communication to the world at large.

When We Dead Awaken is an unforgiving account of the last days of a world-renowned artist, not unlike Ibsen himself. Rubek, an aging sculptor, has lost all interest in the world around him. In spite of his wealth, his fame, and the attentions of his beautiful, young wife, he can find no joy in his banal existence. He has lost interest even in his work, sculpting nothing but occasional portrait busts for wealthy aristocrats whom he despises. He is stagnating, like the murky, shallow waters he travels with his wife . . . trapped in a spiritual vacuum.

MAIA: You've lost all pleasure in your work. You used to take such joy in it—slaving away from morning to night!

RUBEK: Used to . . . yes.

MAIA: But ever since you finished your masterpiece—

RUBEK: *[With disgust.]* My "masterpiece!" Hah!

MAIA: Why are you so bitter? That sculpture has gone round the entire world! It's made you famous!

RUBEK: That sculpture is the very cause of my misfortune, Maia.

MAIA: The very cause of your . . . how can . . . Rubek, it was your greatest triumph! Your crowning achievement! All the critics say so!

RUBEK: What do they know?

MAIA: Well, I should think their opinion would count for *something*.

RUBEK: They're a bunch of pompous windbags! The whole lot of them! They look at my work and . . . and see something that isn't there—something that was never in my mind at all! It's just a bunch of academic nonsense. Why should I expose myself to such ignorance?

MAIA: So it's better to do nothing at all but the occasional portrait bust?

RUBEK: *[A sly smile.]* Oh, my dear little Maia . . . they are not exactly "portrait busts."

At this point, the reader may lift a questioning glance—"Oh, my dear little Maia . . . they are not exactly 'portrait busts.'" Is it possible that Ibsen is speaking of himself? Could Rubek the sculptor be nothing more than a thin disguise for Ibsen the dramatist?

Impatiently, the reader continues.

RUBEK: On the surface, yes, I'll admit I give them the "striking likeness" they so desperately desire, that they gape at in astonishment, but I could never satisfy myself with such a simple task—you should realize that by now.

MAIA: I don't understand.

RUBEK: Well, I have to do something to entertain myself—don't I? So I take a few . . . artistic liberties, let's say . . . make a few embellishments here and there . . . leave a little something hidden in each one, something cryptic, lurking behind those lifelike masks, a subliminal suggestion that my wealthy benefactors are either too stupid or too proud to discern. But someday, perhaps . . . someday, they shall see it. As they huddle round these "portrait busts," as you call them, with their children and their grandchildren, they shall suddenly come to the horrific realization that, at bottom, they are all a bunch of pompous horse-faces, lop-eared dog-skulls, and fatted swine-snouts!

MAIA: You don't mean . . . you haven't literally—

RUBEK: Oh, quite literally. Horse-faces, dog-skulls, and swine-snouts. And it is these double-faced works of art that our excellent plutocrats come and order of me, and pay for in good round figures!

In an article written shortly after his death, there is the following description of Ibsen's study table:

> On the table beside his inkstand was a small tray. Its contents were extraordinary—some little carved wooden Swiss bears, a diminutive black devil, small cats, dogs, and rabbits made of copper, one of which was playing a violin.

> "I never write a single line of any of my dramas unless that tray and its occupants are before me on the table," Ibsen said. "It may seem strange—perhaps it is—but I cannot write without them. Why I use them is my own secret." And he laughed quietly.

Were they his models—these tiny, uncanny creatures—symbols of the souls of men and women and inspiration for his marvelous "portrait busts" with their outer appearance of commonplace, everyday life? Are these animalistic figures, these horse-faces, dog-skulls and swine-snouts, the primitive elements of human nature which society has trapped and imprisoned in the diabolic net of convention, leering at one through the meshes of Ibsen's plays—these commonplace, realistic plays—these portrait busts?

Oh, my dear little Maia . . . they are not exactly "portrait busts."

One has suspected it, all along, through the maze of plays—a certain sinister delight in the dramatist, a quiet chuckling at our inability to divine his meaning. And now, at the end of his career, grown bold, he seems to flaunt it in our very faces as we stand and "gape in astonishment."

I could never satisfy myself with such a simple task—you should realize that by now.

It is his final word—a half-hidden message addressed to generations yet unborn—to the enlightened generation that will no longer stand and gape in astonishment at the striking likeness, for to them the likeness will be of no account.

Those of whom he drew the likeness will be dead and gone; and they—those coming generations—will demand that the artist account for himself.

"Why did you abandon your high calling of poet to work upon these portrait busts? It was not poverty that drove you, nor greed—surely not a desire to live comfortably—you who might have been the greatest poet of your age!"

It is before this tribunal that Ibsen speaks. *When We Dead Awaken* is his defense.

After years of waste and atrophy, Rubek the sculptor finds himself suddenly jolted out of his stupor by an unexpected reunion with Irene, a model who once posed for him and whom he idolized. She is now half-mad—or appears to be so—and literally believes herself to be a walking corpse, a dead woman who roams the earth, who has returned from "the uttermost regions"—from "the great dead waste." In spite of her delusions, however, and in spite of his marriage, Rubek attempts to rekindle the relationship. In his youth, when he had planned his masterpiece, *The Resurrection Day*, Irene had embodied for him all the beauty and goodness of the world, but she has come to despise Rubek in the years since they last met.

IRENE: You did me a great injustice. A passionate young woman . . . full of life and . . . natural desires . . . I stood before you in complete and utter nakedness . . . sacrificed myself for your art . . . and you . . . you—!

Rubek protests that he never did her any wrong, but Irene continues, years of pent-up anger boiling to the surface:

IRENE: You did wrong to my innermost, most inborn nature! I served you with all the pulsing blood of my youth! Fell down at your feet and served you! Exposed myself to you unreservedly! My body! My heart! And not once—not once did you touch me! Not once did you give any part of yourself to me!

In Rubek's original conception, *The Resurrection Day* was to be rendered as "an innocent young woman, not yet corrupted by life, awakening to light and glory without having to put away from her anything ugly or impure." When he first found Irene, he knew at once that he would make use of her for his great work, for she was the perfect representation of this ideal. She served him well during the days of creation that followed, freely sacrificing herself, for she loved the artist. But when the sculpture stood complete, transfigured in the light, Irene slipped into darkness, for she realized at last that Rubek had only used her for his art.

IRENE: Do you remember what you said—the day you finished?

RUBEK: No. What did I say?

IRENE: *[Astonished.]* You don't remember?

RUBEK: I . . . I'm sorry. My mind isn't what it used to be.

IRENE: You took my hands and pressed them to you. And I waited. I waited, Arnold. Breathless. For what seemed like an eternity, I waited! And then you said to me, "Thank you. Thank you, Irene. This has been a priceless episode."

RUBEK: Did I really say that? *Episode? [Pause.]* I'm sure I didn't mean—

IRENE: At that word, I left you.

RUBEK: You take everything so painfully to heart.

IRENE: And you take nothing.

This same innocent muse, this model of goodness and beauty, the spirit of Love and Idealism, came to Ibsen, also, in his youth. Filled with her inspiration, he planned and carried out the great love of his life—his poetic dramas. The beauty of Love, the power of Love, and the ultimate, wonderful resurrection of Love on the earth—these are the themes of the great song that ends with *Brand* and *Peer Gynt.* Then, because he loved not Love for herself, because he did not need her for himself, but only as an inspiration for his art, she left him, cold and desolate and uninspired. He searched for her everywhere, as the sculptor searches for Irene, but she had gone from him. The man who will be merely an artist, shall be artist and nothing more. Love will not serve those who do not live for her, and in her, and to whom she is not the breath of life. Only too late does Rubek realize his error.

RUBEK: When you left . . . when you disappeared . . . I cannot express to you . . . I was filled with such regret. I became painfully aware of all that I had left unsaid . . . all the moments I had allowed to pass . . . without . . . without grasping them . . . without . . . I had come to think of you as something sacred, you see . . . something holy . . . a gift from God . . . a creature of innocence not to be touched save in adoring thoughts. A superstition took hold of me that if I touched you . . . if I desired you with my senses . . . my soul would be desecrated, and I would not be able to finish my work. I was a fool! An idealistic young fool! I should have taken you in my arms right then and there—on the floor of my studio, I should have taken you! With the clay still on my fingers! It would only have added to the beauty of the child—to the depth and complexity of her meaning—of her mystery.

In his loneliness the sculptor weds Maia; in Ibsen's despair when the spirit of Love has left him, when he can no longer, through her inspiration, see beautiful poetic visions, he comes to terms with the spirit of Realism—it was not an easy or natural adjustment on either side. He had known that he ought not to wed her. But he was very desolate. The spirit of Love had left him. He could no longer see beauty in the world, nor idealism, nor poetry. Only Truth remained—realistic, stark truth. Perhaps he could live with her and forget. So they had joined their lives.

The decade from 1867 to 1877 marks a transitional period in Ibsen's career. With the exception of his *Emperor and Galilean*—which was the mere elaboration of a sketch made in Rome some years before—he produced no art-work from the writing of *The Young Men's League*, which he began in 1868, to the presentation of *Pillars of Society* in 1877. Up to this period he had produced, from the time he was twenty years old, an almost regular succession of dramatic works of highly romantic character; after this period, from 1877 to 1899, he produced every other year a play of the most realistic nature, often dealing with some issue of social or political reform—each play belonging to the same order, and the whole differing in every regard from the work of his earlier period. They make in all a dozen plays that are perhaps the most significant dramatic work, artistically, of the nineteenth century.

Ibsen had faced squarely about. He forswore the gods of his youth and waited ten years for the dawning of a new hierarchy. He worked twenty years, now he waited ten, and again he wrought twenty. That is the sum of his life-work, fitting itself, neatly, into decades for the pleasure of the curious. The work of the first twenty years is of the most ultra-romantic character. All literature would have to be searched to find a companion piece for *Peer Gynt* in its romantic emphasis. The plays of this earlier period—which are romantic and poetic and highly artistic—deal, for the most part, with the past. The plays of the second period—which are realistic and written in prose—deal entirely with issues of the present. A change of artistic ideal had taken place in the soul of the poet. Ibsen's realistic work is even more perfect and finished than his romantic. It is as if, when a young man, he had engaged in literature through mere overflow of spirit, a kind of Viking energy that must expend itself—in historical romance, in Norse fancy, in finished phrase, and hurried, tumbling rhymes and lines—work so spontaneous and intricate and finished that it has taxed translators to the utmost to give a conception of its free, bubbling nature and exact perfection of form. Then there came a pause. The artist seemed to hesitate. He planned a new play, *The Young Men's League*. It would be very different from his previous work—it would be in prose, and it would deal with Norwegian society of the present day. *The Young Men's League* has, in itself, no real interest. It is prosaic, hard, and unconvincing. Biographically it has the greatest interest. In it Ibsen tried and failed. Ten years earlier he had made a similar attempt at the prose form in *Love's Comedy*, a satiric drama treating of modern society. Failing to satisfy himself—failing in realism, that is—he afterwards embarked on a massive revision of the play, turning the whole bodily into verse, sometimes line for line and sometimes with free hand. He had recognized that prose is the form best suited to the treatment of modern life, and prose he could not yet handle; therefore he returned to verse. But now, ten years later, a change had come over him. Faced once again with failure, he would not return to the old form and he could not go on. Therefore he waited. The poet stayed his hand, in the main, for almost a decade. And when, at last, he returned to the old battlefield it was with new weapons and in new armor. He had made an uneasy peace with Realism. But it was a marriage of convenience, for she was not his first love.

When We Dead Awaken opens with Rubek and Maia—the uninspired artist and his young wife with her lively, mocking eyes—facing each other wearily across the breakfast table after four or five long years of marriage. Maia knows that she no longer satisfies her husband and senses intuitively that the relationship is in jeopardy.

MAIA: *[Pauses, considering her words carefully.]* There seems to be such an expression of . . . fatigue . . . of utter weariness in your eyes when you condescend, every now and then, to glance in my direction . . . this evil look . . . as if you were nursing some dark plot against me.

Although she chastises Rubek for his emotional withdrawal, Maia has grown weary as well—weary of her husband's artistic temperament, of his moodiness and his lack of attention. As a vital young woman, she has needs of her own—needs which have gone unnoticed by the self-absorbed sculptor.

MAIA: You've been simply dreadful! Crawling off into your cave all the time . . . staying up until all hours of the night . . . you can't say two words to me without slipping into a coma. Sometimes I feel as if I didn't even exist at all! As if I were a figment of my own imagination!

The distance between husband and wife is enormous, a gaping abyss. In only a few years of marriage, they have settled into a mechanical, complacent, and unfulfilling existence, as dysfunctional as it is wearisome. Each secretly longs for a companion who will better understand their particular needs and dreams. The return of Irene is merely the catalyst that forces the issue. After his vision of the white figure in the garden, Rubek is finally compelled to address the situation.

RUBEK: You said this morning that I have become very restless as of late. What do you think might be the reason for that?

MAIA: How should I know? Perhaps you've grown tired of me.

RUBEK: Perhaps.

MAIA: *[Rising angrily.]* If you want to get rid of me, all you have to do is say so!

RUBEK: Sit down.

MAIA: I will not! If you want to have done with me, please say so right out, and I will go this instant!

RUBEK: Do you intend that as a threat, Maia?

MAIA: Yes! *[A short pause.]* No. *[She sits.]* There can be no threat for you in that.

[Pause.]

RUBEK: We cannot possibly go on living like this.

MAIA: No.

RUBEK: What has become so painfully clear these past few months, is that I require a . . . a confidante . . . someone to share all my victories and my defeats—

MAIA: Don't I do that?

RUBEK: Not in the sense that . . . what I need is the companionship of an . . . an equal, so to speak.

MAIA: An equal?

RUBEK: One who can . . . complete me . . . supply in me what is wanting . . . be one with me in all my striving.

MAIA: I can see that you have someone specific in mind.

RUBEK: You can see that, can you?

MAIA: I know you better than you think, Rubek.

She, for her part is deeply offended. He has never dealt fairly with her. She has her own possibilities—possibilities that can never be fully realized in the poet's comfortable home. She, too, longs for the high places. But he will never take her there. In his heart of hearts he despises her. She belongs to the bear-hunter, the great Russian. With him she can be her beautiful free self.

MAIA: Do you remember what you promised me?

RUBEK: What?

MAIA: The day we came to an understanding on our . . .

RUBEK: Our little arrangement?

MAIA: Yes. I promised to go abroad with you . . . to be your constant companion in all things . . . to give myself to you completely . . . and do you remember what you promised me in return?

RUBEK: No.

MAIA: *No? [RUBEK shrugs.]* You promised to take me to the highest mountain and show me all the glory of the world.

RUBEK: *[Laughs.]* Did I? Did I really?!

MAIA: *[Angry at his laughter.]* Yes! All the glory of the world!

RUBEK: Well, Maia . . . you must understand . . . that was merely a . . . a practiced speech . . . a monologue I was once in the habit of performing.

MAIA: Who else did you make such promises to?!

RUBEK: No, you don't understand. It's the sort of thing I used to shout when
          I wanted to lure the neighborhood children out to play in the woods
          and on the mountains.

MAIA: Perhaps you only wanted to lure me out to play as well?

[Pause.]

RUBEK: You must admit, Maia, it has been a tolerably amusing game.

MAIA: More amusing for you, perhaps, than for me.

RUBEK: Oh, you knew very well what you were getting yourself into. You can't
          say that I've treated you badly.

MAIA: You never took me to the highest mountain, and you never showed
          me—

RUBEK: —all the glory of the world? No. I did not. But let me tell you
          something, little Maia—you were not born to climb mountains.

She has never belonged to the artist. She could not stay with him contentedly,
though he has introduced her to polite society and given her all the trinkets and
baubles that wealth can provide. Ibsen has polished Realism, given her all the
advantages of art; but in his heart of hearts he has never truly been inspired by her;
he has always longed for his first love, for the bubbling poetry of his youth.

RUBEK: Let me tell you something, little Maia—you were not born to climb
          mountains.

Rubek watches Maia go with only the slightest sigh, for the other has returned to
him. The Spirit of Love—of beauty and poetry and idealism—has come again out
of the past, to seek him. She is like a dead person, it is true. But she has returned
nonetheless and holds the promise of a reawakening for the sculptor. They talk
together of the past. Rubek communes in his heart with the Spirit that left him
so long ago. She will never leave him again. He will cherish her in his heart, warm
her there, hold her fast to the end. He attempts to explain his artistic development
and the evolution of the sculpture that brought them together—the sculpture
Irene stubbornly refers to as their "child."

RUBEK: I looked at the world around me . . . and I had no choice but to include what I saw. Women and men as I knew them in real life.

IRENE: Others—with our child?! Strangers?!

RUBEK: At the base of the sculpture, I created fissures in the ground, and from this hell-mouth, there are now men and women with dimly-suggested animal faces, swarming up around the child, pulling her down as she tries to rise up into the heavens.

IRENE: My eternal soul . . . you and I . . . we . . . we and our child . . . we lived in that solitary figure!

RUBEK: Yes—we! *We!* I had to include myself, you see. I had to put a little bit of myself into the girl—that glorious figure who can't quite free herself from this earth—who reaches with her hands for the heavens, for perfection, tortured by the knowledge that she will never attain her goal, never escape, that she will remain forever imprisoned in this . . . this hell!

The history of Rubek might be that of Ibsen's own soul. The reader has, almost, a sense of voyeurism, of having come upon something in a deceased relative's chest—among his private papers—something intended, not for the eyes of those who knew him, but only for the eyes of his spiritual children, and for those—long after his death. It is a confession of failure, utter and humiliating.

The autobiographical note is not forced, but one may easily read it between the lines. It is Ibsen's life history—the spontaneous, bubbling delight in his early work when the Spirit of Love possessed him—the very essence of *Peer Gynt* testifies to it. The free rollicking metre and the lines that have taxed translators to the utmost reveal the soul of the poet in love with his work and working with spontaneous touch. The theme is ever the divine power of Love that must dawn at last upon the earth. Then—when *Peer Gynt* was done—the anxious halting pause that came in his work, his fumbling attempt at prose in *The Young Men's League*, and the revision of his earlier work—all the time searching for the Spirit that had left him, and without whom he finds himself powerless to create. He takes up *Emperor and Galilean.* The form is poetical, but the soul of poetry is not there. It has escaped him forever. He will never find it again. He knows it now. *The Emperor and Galilean* has taught him the truth. It stands there in the midst of his work, a great, bare, pretentious thing—neither prose nor poetry. Despair is in his heart. He stays his hand. His work is done.

There is still the desire in his heart, the necessity in his nature to create, but he is sterile. He can no longer make poems. The Spirit has left him. Beauty has gone from the world, and taken idealism with it. The world is a cold, barren place, with only men and women, ugly and hard and prosaic, leering at him. Then comes the whisper in his ear. They throng upon his soul, these men and women of the real world, hard and cruel and cunning. His keen eyes pierce them to their very souls, as through transparent walls of glass. Why should he not write of them as he sees them—reveal them to themselves? He writes *Pillars of Society*. On the pedestal of his life-work, he creates a fissure in the ground, and from this hell-mouth "men and women with dimly-suggested animal faces" begin to swarm up. *A Doll's House* follows and *Ghosts, An Enemy of the People, The Wild Duck, Rosmersholm, The Lady from the Sea*. The group is complete at last, and he gives it to the world. The world praises him and blames him, but for the most part, it admires the skill, "the striking likeness." His later works are primarily portrait plays, thrown off from time to time to satisfy his need to create. There is no higher unity that binds them together as a group. With *John Gabriel Borkman* he finds that even this sort of work is no longer possible, and he senses that the time has come at last to throw off his shackles, for he has already had a vision of a white figure walking in the garden—a vision that cannot be fully realized unless the dramatist once again girds himself in the old armor, takes up the weapons of his youth.

RUBEK: I've grown quite fond of you, Maia. I have. And I don't want you to feel as if you've failed in any way. On the contrary, you've been a delightful companion. But I have found myself sinking, more and more, into long periods of darkness. And what I've come to realize is this: I am simply not suited for the leisurely pursuit of happiness. Life doesn't shape itself that way for me. I must go on working, you see—producing one work of art after another—right up until my dying day, or else I will simply waste away.

MAIA: What does that have to do with—

RUBEK: Madame von Satow?

MAIA: I was going to say with me.

RUBEK: *[Pauses, laying a hand on his breast.]* In here, you see—in here I have a little lock-box . . . and in that box are stored up all my sculptor's visions . . . inspirations for all my future works. When she left, Madame von Satow, when she disappeared without a trace, the lock of that box snapped shut. She had the key, you see—she took it with her—so all of those visions, they were left unrealized. All of those treasures—wasted. The years pass, and I have no means of getting at them. I can only fumble at the lock.

MAIA: Didn't I inspire you at all, Rubek? Even a little bit?

RUBEK: You reminded me of her . . . of Irene, as she once was . . . years ago. You are more alike than you might suspect. That's what drew me to you. But you, little Maia . . . you had no key.

[Pause.]

MAIA: Then you must get her to open this box for you. You make such a fuss over the simplest things.

Surprisingly, she is not jealous of returning love.

MAIA: I'm sure in town—in that great big house of ours—surely there must be room enough for three.

RUBEK: For three?

MAIA: That's right.

RUBEK: You mean—

MAIA: I'm sure we can still be of some use to one another. And if it doesn't work out, well, we will simply get out of each other's way—part entirely. No need to be anxious about that.

Surely in all the poet's great house—in all Ibsen's work—there must be room for Realism and Idealism, too. If not, then Realism will gladly take her leave. She will be free. It is her nature. Forms and bonds weary her. She has never lived with him joyously. He has made too formal, too artistic a thing of her.

In its outward form and its use of prose, *When We Dead Awaken* resembles Ibsen's later plays, but in tone and spirit, it is not far removed from the plays of his youth. It is, in a sense a fusion of his two periods. A harbinger of the symbolist movement in Europe, this "dramatic epilogue" suggests that, had Ibsen lived, he might have moved into yet another period of development, a third period in which he combined the poetic vitality of his early work with the realistic trappings and refined form of his later dramas.

For its personal interest, namely, as the grand poetical confession of a great artist's lifelong struggle to find balance in his art and his life, this play stands supreme. It interweaves nearly all the leading motifs by which Ibsen's life and work were governed. But through the maze of harmonies a final melody rings clearly forth—the remorseful query: What shall it profit a man to enrich the whole world if by so doing he squanders his own existence? While the great artist labors and suffers in isolation, the world moves relentlessly forward, heedless of his dreams and aspirations. And is it not, after all, the part of wisdom to heed the Mephistophelian advice:

> My worthy friend, gray are all theories,
> And green alone Life's golden tree.

But how shall we dead awaken in this world? How shall we shock ourselves out of an existence that has become trite, mechanical, complacent and uninspired?

> I should have taken you in my arms right then and there—on
> the floor of my studio, I should have taken you! With the clay
> still on my fingers! It would only have added to the beauty of
> the child—to the depth and complexity of her meaning—of
> her mystery.

Ibsen seems to echo the assertion of D.H. Lawrence that "Love is the flower of life, and blossoms unexpectedly and without law, and must be plucked where it is found, and enjoyed for the brief hour of its duration." Nothing, he seems to say, must stand in the way of love, not even art. And yet his protagonist is unable to part completely with his artistic dreams. Even on the mountain-top he clings to them. Even as death approaches. Perhaps Ibsen, too, as he wrote his final play, as he felt his mind slipping into darkness, was torn.

When We Dead Awaken contains many flashes of Ibsen's brilliance—yet it is generally considered the product of a failing mind. This is not because of any falling off in the dramatic power of Ibsen's storytelling—his conception is superb. The story is compelling and charged with meaning. The characters are complex and human. No, the weaknesses in this drama are merely a function of the execution—it was here that Ibsen's seventy-year-old mind stumbled. His "dramatic epilogue" contains excess dialogue, half-sounded chords of thematic development, and repetitive beats which weaken and mask the true power of this haunting play—yet beneath is a masterpiece struggling to emerge from the raw material, from the clay of Ibsen's still-fertile imagination. Like a paleontologist attempting to unearth an ancient fossil from the earth and rock where it has lain for thousands of years, carefully reconstructing the skeleton where it has been worn away by time and the elements, so this adaptation attempts to brush away the dust from this misunderstood drama—to separate the wheat from the chaff so to speak—to tighten the dramatic structure and complete the thematic chords while remaining true to the original conception, at last restoring Ibsen's final apocalyptic vision to its rightful place among his greatest plays.

WALTER WYKES & JENNETTE LEE

CHARACTERS

Arnold Rubek: A sculptor
Maia Rubek: His wife.
Mr. Ulfheim: A bear-hunter.
Irene von Satow: A former model
Inspector
Sister of Mercy

PLACE

Norway: The Bath Hotel. A mountain retreat. A mountain-side.

TIME: 1899

ACT I

[Outside the Bath Hotel. Two figures sit beside a covered table, each holding a newspaper. PROFESSOR RUBEK, a rather distinguished-looking, elderly gentleman, is engrossed in his reading, but MAIA, much younger and very pretty, sits pouting with her paper folded in her lap. She stares at RUBEK—as if waiting for him to speak. He does not. She lets out a deep sigh. RUBEK ignores this. She, very deliberately, sighs again. Nothing.]

MAIA
[In frustration.]
Oh!
[Throws her newspaper to the ground.]
How can you just sit there?! It's unbearable! This . . . this silence!
[RUBEK continues to read.]
Rubek!
[RUBEK continues to read.]
Rubek, say something! Say something, or I swear I'll—

RUBEK
[Still reading.]
You don't seem entirely happy to be home, Maia.

MAIA
Are you?
[No response.]
Well? Are you, Professor—happy to be home?

RUBEK
Not entirely. No.

MAIA

There! You see! I knew it! I hate it when you're unhappy! We'll go away! Tonight! As soon as possible!

RUBEK

You really are a strange little person.

MAIA

Am I? *Strange?* Because I'm not happy moping around up here?

RUBEK

Which of us was it that insisted on coming north for the summer?
[No response.]
It was certainly not I.

MAIA

Well . . . who could have known that everything would have changed so much? It's only been four years since I went away!

RUBEK

I?

MAIA

[Quickly.]
We.
[Pause.]

RUBEK

Perhaps it's not the place that's changed.

MAIA

What's that supposed to mean?

RUBEK

Well, Maia . . . you have become accustomed to a very different way of life than what you were used to at home.

MAIA

And?

RUBEK

And . . . well . . . I suppose what I'm trying to say is—

MAIA

I'm the one that's changed?! Just me?! Not these people?!

RUBEK

The people too, yes, a little—and not at all in the direction one might prefer—I'll give you that.

MAIA

I should think so!

RUBEK

But *you* must admit, Maia, that . . .
[*He pauses . . . shakes his head.*]
No. Never mind.
[*He forces a faint smile and returns to his paper.*]

MAIA

What?
[*Pause.*]
What were you going to say?

RUBEK

Nothing. There's no point in continuing this conversation. No good can come of it. Tomorrow we will pack our bags and board that great luxurious steamer in the harbor there. We'll sail round the coast, straight out to the polar sea, and everything will be much more pleasant.

MAIA

Well . . . all right. If it will make you happy.

RUBEK
[*Astonished.*]
Me?

MAIA

That's right.
[*RUBEK laughs.*]

29

now Rubek—I may not have the benefit of your superior education, but I am a woman, after all. I can certainly tell when something's wrong—and you have been quite miserable as of late.

RUBEK

Have I?

MAIA

You've been simply dreadful! Crawling off into your cave all the time . . . staying up until all hours of the night . . . you can't say two words to me without slipping into a coma. Sometimes I feel as if I didn't even exist at all! As if I were a figment of my own imagination!

RUBEK
[Somewhat playful.]
Is my little companion feeling neglected?

MAIA

It's not just me. You've lost all pleasure in your work. You used to take such joy in it—slaving away from morning to night!

RUBEK

Used to . . . yes.

MAIA

But ever since you finished your masterpiece—

RUBEK
[With disgust.]
My "masterpiece!" Hah!

MAIA

Why are you so bitter? That sculpture has gone round the entire world! It's made you famous!

RUBEK

That sculpture is the very cause of my misfortune, Maia.

MAIA

The very cause of your . . . how can . . . Rubek, it was your greatest triumph! Your crowning achievement! All the critics say so!

RUBEK

What do they know?

MAIA

Well, I should think their opinion would count for *something*.

RUBEK

They're a bunch of pompous windbags! The whole lot of them! They look at my work and . . . and see something that isn't there—something that was never in my mind at all! It's just a bunch of academic nonsense. Why should I expose myself to such ignorance?

MAIA

So it's better to do nothing at all but the occasional portrait bust?

RUBEK

[A sly smile.]
Oh, my dear little Maia . . . they are not exactly "portrait busts."

MAIA

No? What would you call them?

RUBEK

On the surface, yes, I'll admit I give them the "striking likeness" they so desperately desire, that they gape at in astonishment, but I could never satisfy myself with such a simple task—you should realize that by now.

MAIA

I don't understand.

RUBEK

Well, I have to do something to entertain myself—don't I? So I take a few . . . artistic liberties, let's say . . . make a few embellishments here and there . . . leave a little something hidden in each one, something cryptic, lurking behind those lifelike masks, a subliminal suggestion that my wealthy benefactors are either too stupid or too proud to discern. But someday, perhaps . . . someday, they shall see it. As they huddle round these "portrait busts," as you call them, with their children and their grandchildren, they shall suddenly come to the horrific realization that, at bottom, they are all a bunch of pompous horse-faces, lop-eared dog-skulls, and fatted swine-snouts!

MAIA

You don't mean . . . you haven't literally—

RUBEK

Oh, quite literally. Horse-faces, dog-skulls, and swine-snouts. And it is these double-faced works of art that our excellent plutocrats come and order of me, and pay for in good round figures!

MAIA

Oh, Rubek! How perfect! Bravo!
[MAIA claps, delighted.]
When you talk like this, it . . . it reminds me of the old days.
[She fills his glass.]
Come! Drink and be happy!

RUBEK

I am happy, Maia. In a way. There is, after all, a certain contentment that comes from having at one's disposal everything one could possibly wish for . . . all outward things.
[Pause.]
Don't you agree?

[Silence.]

MAIA

Do you remember what you promised me?

RUBEK

What?

MAIA

The day we came to an understanding on our . . .

RUBEK

Our little arrangement?

MAIA

Yes. I promised to go abroad with you . . . to be your constant companion in all things . . . to give myself to you completely . . . and do you remember what you promised me in return?

RUBEK

No.

MAIA

No?

[*RUBEK shrugs.*]
You promised to take me to the highest mountain and show me all the glory of the world.

RUBEK

[*Laughs.*]
Did I? Did I really?!

MAIA

[*Angry at his laughter.*]
Yes! All the glory of the world!

RUBEK

Well, Maia . . . you must understand . . . that was merely a . . . a practiced speech . . . a monologue I was once in the habit of performing.

MAIA

Who else did you make such promises to?!

RUBEK

No, you don't understand. It's the sort of thing I used to shout when I wanted to lure the neighborhood children out to play in the woods and on the mountains.

MAIA

Perhaps you only wanted to lure me out to play as well?
[*Pause.*]

RUBEK

You must admit, Maia, it has been a tolerably amusing game.

MAIA

More amusing for you, perhaps, than for me.

RUBEK

Oh, you knew very well what you were getting yourself into. You can't say that I've treated you badly.

33

MAIA

You never took me to the highest mountain, and you never showed me—

RUBEK

—all the glory of the world? No. I did not. But let me tell you something, little Maia—you were not born to climb mountains.

MAIA

There was a time when you thought I was.

RUBEK

Perhaps.

MAIA

Have things really changed so much? Has it been such a terribly long time?

RUBEK

It is beginning, now, to seem a trifle long—yes.

MAIA

Oh! A *trifle long*, is it?! Well . . . I shall bore you no longer!
>   *[MAIA returns to the table and buries herself in her newspaper. After a few moments, THE INSPECTOR enters from his rounds in the park. He wears gloves and carries a stick.]*

INSPECTOR
[Taking off his hat.]
Good morning, Mrs. Rubek. Professor.

RUBEK

Good morning, Inspector.

INSPECTOR

May I be so bold as to inquire how you slept?

MAIA

Like a stone. Aside from my husband's snoring and his constant trips to the bathroom, everything was quite perfect. But that must be expected from a man of his age.

INSPECTOR

I see ... well ... the ... ahh ... the first night in a strange place can be rather trying.

[Pause.]

And the professor?

RUBEK

Oh, I never get much sleep ... especially as of late.

INSPECTOR

I'm sorry to hear that. Nevertheless, I suspect, after a few weeks here at the Baths, you will be sleeping just as soundly as your lovely young wife.

RUBEK

One can only hope.

[An awkward pause.]

INSPECTOR

Well ... if there's anything I can do to make your stay more pleasant, please don't hesitate to ask.

MAIA

That's very nice of you.

RUBEK

Tell me, Inspector ... I'm curious ... are any of your patients in the habit of visiting the baths at night.

INSPECTOR

At night? No.

RUBEK

No?

INSPECTOR

Certainly not.

RUBEK

Is there someone, then, who might be in the habit of walking about the park at night?

INSPECTOR

I'm afraid that isn't allowed.

MAIA

I told you.

INSPECTOR

What is this all about?

RUBEK

When I woke up last night, I looked out the window and caught a glimpse of a white figure out there among the trees.

INSPECTOR

A white figure?

MAIA

You must have dreamt it. Or imagined it entirely. His eyes aren't what they used to be.

RUBEK

I did not dream it! There was a white figure. A woman. Then, after her, came another—quite dark—like a shadow.

INSPECTOR

A dark one?

RUBEK

Yes.

INSPECTOR

Just behind the white figure? At her heels?

RUBEK

Yes—at a little distance.

INSPECTOR
[Very pleased with himself.]
I believe I can explain the mystery. We have a certain guest—a foreigner. She's rented that little pavilion there. Slender. Very pale. Wanders about in a constant daze, as if she didn't even see the rest of us, although she can't be blind because

she finds her way well enough. At any rate, she is always wrapped in a large white shawl.

RUBEK
It must have been her. And the dark figure?

INSPECTOR
She is always accompanied by a Sister of Mercy, in black, with a silver cross hanging from her neck.

RUBEK
Ah-hah! Then I'm not crazy after all!

INSPECTOR
I should say not. They came from abroad about a week ago.

RUBEK
What is the lady's name?

INSPECTOR
She registered herself as "Madame von Satow, with companion." We know nothing more.

RUBEK
[To himself.]
Satow? Satow—?

INSPECTOR
Do you know someone of that name, Professor?

RUBEK
No one. Satow? Sounds Russian. Or Slavonic, at any rate. What language does she speak?

INSPECTOR
When the two women speak together, it's a language I can't make out at all. But to the rest of us, she speaks Norwegian like a native.

RUBEK
Norwegian? Are you sure?

MAIA
[Without looking up from her paper.]
How could he be mistaken in that?

RUBEK
You've heard her yourself?

INSPECTOR
Several times. Only a few words—she doesn't speak much—but—

RUBEK
But it was Norwegian?

INSPECTOR
Very good Norwegian. With a touch of north-country accent, I believe.

RUBEK
That too!

MAIA
Perhaps this lady was one of your models, Professor. You are said to have had so many models—in your younger days, I mean.

RUBEK
[Very sharply.]
I had only one model! One and one only—for everything I have done!
[An awkward pause.]

INSPECTOR
If you will excuse me, I think I'll take my leave. I see a certain guest approaching whom it is not particularly agreeable to meet. Especially in the presence of a lady.

RUBEK
Who is it?

INSPECTOR
A Mr. Ulfheim.

RUBEK
Ahh—yes.

INSPECTOR

The bear-killer, as they call him.

RUBEK

I'm quite familiar with the man.

INSPECTOR

My apologies.

RUBEK

Is he on your list of patients.

INSPECTOR

Thankfully, no. But he comes through once a year on his way to the hunting-grounds. If you'll excuse me.

[The INSPECTOR begins to exit.]

ULFHEIM

[Offstage.]

Stop there! You! Dammit, stand still, man! Why are you always scuttling off in the opposite direction?!

INSPECTOR

I do not "scuttle."

[Enter ULFHEIM. He has the appearance of a wild man. His hair and beard are matted, and he speaks in a loud voice.]

ULFHEIM

Is this any way to treat guests—scampering off with your tail between your legs?!

INSPECTOR

[Indignant.]

Is there something I can *do* for you, Mr. Ulfheim?

ULFHEIM

My dogs need food.

INSPECTOR

I'll see to it right away.

[The INSPECTOR turns to go.]

ULFHEIM

There he goes again—running off before I'm done with him!

INSPECTOR

I'm sorry—was there something else?

ULFHEIM

Damn right there's something else! Feed them—but not too much! Keep them ravenous! Fresh meat-bones—but just a few scraps of meat—do you hear?! And be sure it's reeking raw and bloody! Oh, and get me some more brandy while your at it. Now to hell with you!

INSPECTOR
[His chin held high.]

As you wish.

[Exit the INSPECTOR. ULFHEIM stares for a moment at MAIA—then notices RUBEK and lifts his hat.]

ULFHEIM

I'll be damned! It looks like I've strayed into tip-top society!

RUBEK

What's that, Mr. Ulfheim?

ULFHEIM
[A hint of sarcasm.]
I believe I have the honor of addressing the great sculptor Rubek!

RUBEK

We have met before, you know.

ULFHEIM

Long time ago. You weren't so famous then. Even a dirty bear-hunter might venture to speak to you.

RUBEK

I don't bite even now.

MAIA
[Intrigued.]
Are you really a bear-hunter?

ULFHEIM

When I have the chance. But I make the best of any game that comes my way—eagles, wolves, women . . . just so it's fresh and juicy and has plenty of blood in it.

MAIA

But you like bear-hunting best.

ULFHEIM

Best—yes. The knife in your hand. The beast writhing beneath you. There's nothing quite like it.

[Pause.]

Well . . . your husband's work, perhaps.

MAIA

My *husband's* work?!

[Laughs.]

Why . . . it's not the same at all!

ULFHEIM

I beg to differ, ma'am. We both work with hard material, your husband and I. I struggle with tense, quivering bear sinews—he with marble blocks. And the stone has something to fight for too, after all—just like the bear when you have him cornered in his lair. It is dead and determined by no means to let itself be hammered into life.

RUBEK

That is a very astute analogy, Mr. Ulfheim.

ULFHEIM

Glad you approve.

MAIA

Are you going up into the forest now—to hunt?

ULFHEIM

The mountains. You see that peak there—rising above everything else?

MAIA

The highest one?

ULFHEIM

That's where I'm going.

MAIA

How exciting!

ULFHEIM

Have you ever been to the mountains?

MAIA

Never.

ULFHEIM

Well, you should come! I'll take you! You and the Professor, if you like.

MAIA

Do you think I'd make a good mountain-climber, Mr. Ulfheim?

ULFHEIM

The prettiest mountain-climber I've ever seen.

MAIA

Did you hear that, Rubek?

RUBEK

Yes. Unfortunately, we've already made plans for a sea voyage this summer—round the coast—through the island channels.

ULFHEIM

Ugh! What in god's name do you want with those damnable sickly gutters?! No, much better to come with me to the mountains—breathe the clean air—sleep beneath the stars. We'll pitch our tent on the highest peak. You've never seen anything like it—far above the taint of men—it's like—

MAIA

All the glory of the world?

ULFHEIM

Yes! All the glory of the world! That's it exactly!

[*Enter the SISTER OF MERCY. She is hooded—her face is not visible. She looks about for a moment—then enters the hotel. ULFHEIM shudders.*]

Where's the body?

RUBEK

What?

ULFHEIM

That scarecrow doesn't hang about where everyone's fit and healthy. Someone's about to give up the ghost, believe me. And the sooner the better. People who are sick and old should have the decency to get themselves buried as quickly as possible so the rest of us can go on living.

RUBEK

Have you ever been ill yourself, Mr. Ulfheim.

ULFHEIM

Never. If I had, I shouldn't be here. But my closest friends—they have been ill, poor things.

RUBEK

And did you wish them dead, your friends, when they were ill?

ULFHEIM

I did more than that. I helped them along.

RUBEK

Helped them along?

ULFHEIM

That's right.

RUBEK

What do you mean?

ULFHEIM

I shot them.

RUBEK
[Doubtful.]

Shot them?

MAIA

Shot them *dead*?!

ULFHEIM

I never miss.

MAIA

But . . . how can you . . . you can't possibly . . . how can you live with yourself?!
[*ULFHEIM shrugs.*]
You can't just go around shooting people!

ULFHEIM

Not people.

MAIA

But you said—

ULFHEIM

My dogs.

MAIA

Your *dogs*? Dogs are your closest friends? Mr. Ulfheim, that's so sad!

ULFHEIM

Not sad at all. They are honest, trustworthy, completely loyal, and when one of
them turns sick—pow! There's my friend sent packing to the next world.
[*The SISTER OF MERCY returns with a tray of bread
and water. She sets it on a table and exits.*]
There! You see! What did I tell you? That's not food for the living. Bread and
water. It wouldn't sustain a corpse! You should see my comrades feeding. They
swallow great meat-bones whole—gulp them down like ravenous wolves! It's
quite a show. Would you like to watch?

MAIA
[*Smiling at RUBEK.*]

Yes. Yes, I would.

ULFHEIM

Spoken like a woman of true spirit! Come along, then. It'll give us a chance to talk over this trip to the mountains.

> [MAIA and ULFHEIM exit around the corner of the hotel. Almost immediately, IRENE enters from the hotel and seats herself in front of the tray of food. She raises her glass and is about to drink, but stops and stares at RUBEK with a strange, vacant expression. RUBEK stares back at her in disbelief. After a long moment, he rises and approaches her table.]

RUBEK

Irene?

> [Pause.]

Is it . . . is it really you?

> [Pause.]

Don't you recognize me?

> [Pause.]

It's me. Arnold.

> [Pause.]

IRENE

Who was that woman—there at the table?

RUBEK

> [Reluctantly.]

My . . . my wife. Maia.

> [Pause. IRENE stares at him.]

IRENE

She does not concern me.

RUBEK

No—

IRENE

She was taken after my lifetime.

RUBEK

After your—?

IRENE

And the child? I hear the child is prospering.

RUBEK

Oh, yes. The child . . . our child has become famous the world over. I suppose you've read about it.

IRENE

It has made its father famous as well. That was your dream.

RUBEK

I suppose so . . . yes . . . at the time.

IRENE

I should have killed that child.

RUBEK

What—?

IRENE

Killed it before I went away! Crushed it into dust!

RUBEK

I . . . I don't understand. Why would you want to harm the . . . it was as much a part of you as—

IRENE

More! More me than anything!

RUBEK

Yes. All right. More. You're right, of course. I . . . I didn't mean to upset you.
[Pause. He moves closer.]
I can't believe you're really here—right in front of me. I've often wondered what happened to you. You disappeared so suddenly . . . left no trace. I searched for you, but—

IRENE

[A bitter laugh.]

Why?

RUBEK

Why?

IRENE

You no longer had any use for me.

RUBEK

No use for you?

IRENE

Your masterpiece was complete. Your great work! The child stood transfigured in the light. And I slipped into darkness. My work was done. What need could you possibly have had for me then?

RUBEK

How can you ask that?
                    [No response.]
Surely you don't think I would have just . . . abandoned you? Do you? Irene?
                    [No response.]
Surely you know me better than that.
                    [She ignores him. Pause.]
Where did you go? When you left—

IRENE

What does it matter?

RUBEK

I want to know.

IRENE

I've traveled many lands.

RUBEK

How did you survive?

IRENE

A woman can never go hungry if she is willing to make use of her body. You taught me that. I turned the heads of all sorts of men. I did more than that. Much more than I could ever do with you, Arnold. You always kept such a tight lid on yourself.

RUBEK

You married?

IRENE

Yes. I married one of them. A distinguished diplomat. I managed to drive him quite out of his mind. It was great sport.

RUBEK

Where is he now?

IRENE

In a churchyard somewhere. With a fine monument over him and a bullet rattling in his skull.

RUBEK

He killed himself?

[No response.]

I'm so sorry.

IRENE

For what?

RUBEK

The loss. Your husband.

IRENE

[Shrugs.]

There were others to take his place.

RUBEK

Others?

IRENE

My second husband, for one. The Russian.

RUBEK

Satow?

IRENE

Yes.

RUBEK

And where is he?

IRENE

In one of his gold mines.

RUBEK

Ahh. Still living, then.

IRENE

Not exactly—no.

RUBEK

Not exactly?

IRENE

I killed him.

RUBEK

Killed—?

IRENE

Killed him with a fine sharp dagger which I always keep under my pillow.

RUBEK

[Laughs.]

You're trying to frighten me, Irene. I know you better than that—you're not capable of such a thing.

IRENE

No?

RUBEK

No. I wouldn't believe it for a second.

[Pause.]

Did you have any children?

IRENE

I've had many children. With many men.

RUBEK

And where are they—your children?

IRENE

I killed them too.

RUBEK

Preposterous! Now you've gone too far!

IRENE

I killed them, I tell you! Murdered them, one by one, as soon as they came into the world! Slit their little throats with that same sharp dagger! Put them in the ground before they could dirty their lungs on this black air!
[Pause.]

RUBEK

There is something hidden behind everything you say.

IRENE

How can I help that when every word I say is whispered in my ear?!

RUBEK

More riddles. But riddles are meant to be solved, Irene. And I believe I am just the man to divine your meaning. Now, let me have a good look at you.
[He rests his hands on the table and stares at her intently.]
Some of the strings of your nature have been broken.

IRENE

That always happens when a young warm-blooded woman dies.

RUBEK

Dies?

IRENE

Yes. Dies.

RUBEK

So you—

IRENE

I have been dead for many years.

RUBEK

Strange. You appear quite lifelike.

IRENE

Your senses deceive you.

RUBEK

You've a fine complexion for a dead woman. Let me feel your pulse.

IRENE

No! Don't touch me!

RUBEK

Irene . . . stop this foolishness.

IRENE

I could no more stop the moon in its tracks or pluck the stars from the sky. Some things are simply beyond one's control, Arnold. Just as it was beyond my control that night—

RUBEK

What night?

IRENE

—when they came for me—

RUBEK

Who? Who came?

IRENE

—when they bound me . . . laced my arms together . . . lowered me into a grave . . . a dark hole in the ground with iron bars and padded walls . . . and no one on the earth above could hear my screams.

RUBEK

I don't understand. Padded walls? They locked you away? In . . . in an asylum?

IRENE

No! In a grave!

RUBEK

Irene . . . my god . . . if I . . . if I'd only known, I—

IRENE

[Sharply.]
What?! What would you have done?! Come to my *rescue?*

RUBEK

Yes!

IRENE

You? The very cause of my . . .
[Laughs incredulously.]
You forced me into the grave, Arnold! It was your doing!

RUBEK

How can you blame me for your . . . your death, as you call it?

IRENE

Who *else* would I blame?

RUBEK

But . . . I had nothing to do with it.

IRENE

You *did!*

RUBEK

How? In what way? You're the one who disappeared. I had no means of tracking you down. I didn't even know if you were still alive! How could I possibly have been involved in your abduction?
[She glares at him. Silence.]

IRENE

It almost seems like old times—doesn't it? The two of us . . . sitting here . . . together . . . a little ways apart . . . also like old times.

RUBEK

Yes.

IRENE

Yes.

[Pause.]

RUBEK

Of course, there had to be a certain distance then.

IRENE

Was it really necessary?

RUBEK

Yes, I believe it was. At least . . . I believed so, then.

IRENE

And now? What do you believe now?

RUBEK

I don't know.

[Pause.]

IRENE

You did me a great injustice, Arnold. A passionate young woman . . . full of life and . . . natural desires . . . I stood before you in complete and utter nakedness . . . sacrificed myself for your art . . . and you . . . you—!

RUBEK

I never did you any wrong, Irene!

IRENE

You did!

RUBEK

Never!

IRENE

You did wrong to my innermost, most inborn nature! I served you with all the pulsing blood of my youth! Fell down at your feet and served you! Exposed myself to you unreservedly! My body! My heart! And not once—not once did you touch me! Not once did you give any part of yourself to me!

53

RUBEK

I was an artist, Irene.

IRENE

Pah!

RUBEK

I couldn't afford any distractions.

IRENE

Yes! Yes! Always art before life!

RUBEK

I had to finish my—

IRENE

—our child! How can one conceive a child without . . . without touching . . . without feeling the pulse of another! The hot breath of life! What a cold and infertile soul that child must bear!

RUBEK

Judge me as you will, Irene, but at the time I was totally devoted to finishing my life's work.

IRENE

And after that? How many models did you have after me, Arnold? How many other women did you exploit for your art? What poems have you made since? In marble, I mean.

RUBEK

I have made no poems since you left—only wasted my life away.

IRENE

And that woman at the table?

RUBEK

Maia?

[Pause.]

I'd rather not talk about her.

IRENE

I thought as much.

RUBEK

No, no . . . you don't understand.

IRENE

Don't I?

RUBEK

She's . . .

IRENE

What?

RUBEK

She's nothing.

IRENE

Nothing?

RUBEK

No. Only a . . . a plaything.
                    [Pause.]
A distraction.

IRENE

Nothing more?

RUBEK

No. She's a child, for god's sake.
                    [Pause.]
I'm sometimes ashamed of myself.

MAIA
             [Offstage.]
Rubek!
             [Entering around the corner of the hotel.]
Rubek, you may frown as much as you like, but—
             [Seeing IRENE, she pauses.]
Oh . . . I see you've made a friend.

RUBEK

[Bluntly.]

What do you want?

MAIA

I only wanted to say that I have no intention of going with you on that disgusting steamboat. You may do what you like, but *I* am going to the mountains! I've made up my mind, and there's nothing you can do to stop me!

RUBEK

Fine.

MAIA

[Taken aback.]

What?

RUBEK

Fine.

[Pause.]

MAIA

You . . . you really don't care?

RUBEK

You're a grown woman, Maia—do what you like.

MAIA

But—

[Pause.]

RUBEK

Well? What is it? Is something wrong?

MAIA

No. Nothing's wrong.

[Pause.]

I'll inform the bear-killer, at once. He'll be delighted. He tells the most wonderful stories—about life up there! You have no idea! Horrible, ugly, wonderful stories! It's an entirely different world!

[Pause.]

All right, then. If you have no objections, I'll just . . .

[Pause.]

Of course, I have nothing to wear in the mountains. I'll have to buy clothes, and I have nothing left of my allowance.

RUBEK

Have it billed to the room.

[Pause.]

MAIA

Fine.

[MAIA exits into the hotel. Silence.]

IRENE

She knows—that you have no feelings for her?

RUBEK

She has some idea.

IRENE

And you're sending her to the mountains . . . with another man?

RUBEK

Apparently so.

[Pause.]

IRENE

You promised to take me there—once.

RUBEK

Did I?

IRENE

Yes. A long time ago.

RUBEK

Perhaps it's not too late.

IRENE

What?

RUBEK

If you still have any interest . . . perhaps I could arrange a mountain excursion. For the two of us.

IRENE

Perhaps.

[Pause.]

RUBEK

Why did you come back, Irene?

IRENE

I realized I had left something behind. Something indispensable. Something one ought never to part with.

RUBEK

And what was that?

IRENE

My living soul.

[After a moment, the SISTER OF MERCY appears. IRENE rises and exits, followed by the woman in black. RUBEK stares after them.]

*　　*　　*

ACT II

[*A mountain retreat. RUBEK sits quietly on a bench. Children can be heard playing happily in the distance.*]

MAIA
[*Offstage.*]

Rubek! Rubek!

[*She enters, dressed in mountain-climbing attire.*]

There you are. I've been looking all over.

RUBEK

You weren't at dinner.

MAIA

No. We had our dinner in the open air!

RUBEK

We?

MAIA

I and that horrid bear-killer, of course.

RUBEK

Ahh. The bear-killer.

MAIA

And first thing tomorrow, we're off again! It's so exciting! The thrill of the hunt and all that. You have no idea!

RUBEK

Have you found any tracks?

MAIA
[Laughs.]
Tracks?

RUBEK
Bears do leave tracks, I assume?

MAIA
[With a superior tone.]
You don't actually think there are bears prowling about the open mountains—do you?

RUBEK
Where then?

MAIA
Down—far beneath. On the lower slopes. The thickest parts of the forest. Places your ordinary person could never get to.

RUBEK
I see. And that's where you're going tomorrow—the two of you? These isolated slopes?

MAIA
Or perhaps tonight. If you have no objections.

RUBEK
Far be it from me to—

MAIA
Of course Lars goes with us—with the dogs. Lars is his servant boy.

RUBEK
I have no interest in the movements of Mr. Lars and his dogs.
[Pause. The happy laughter of children rises in the distance.]

MAIA
Ugh! How can you tolerate those children's screams?!

RUBEK

I actually find them quite soothing. There's something harmonious—almost musical—in their movements, now and then; amid all the clumsiness.

MAIA
[With a scornful laugh.]
You are always, *always the artist.*

RUBEK

So I've been told.
[Pause.]

MAIA

There's not a bit of the artist in him.

RUBEK

The bear-killer, you mean?

MAIA

That's right. Not the least little bit.

RUBEK

I'm sure you're quite right.

MAIA

And so ugly! Uggh!

RUBEK

Is that why you're so anxious to run off with him?

MAIA

I don't know.
[Pause.]
You're ugly too, Rubek.

RUBEK

You've only just discovered this?
[MAIA shrugs.]
One doesn't grow younger, Frau Maia. One doesn't grow younger.

MAIA

It's not that sort of ugliness I mean.

RUBEK

What then?

MAIA

[Pauses, considering her words carefully.]
There seems to be such an expression of . . . fatigue . . . of utter weariness in your eyes when you condescend, every now and then, to glance in my direction . . . this evil look . . . as if you were nursing some dark plot against me.
[Pause.]

RUBEK

Come here, Maia.
[She doesn't move.]
Come. Sit. I want to talk to you about something.

MAIA

Shall I sit on your knee, like I used to, and let you stroke my hair?

RUBEK

No.

MAIA

Why not?

RUBEK

Maia—

MAIA

[Insistent.]
Why not?

RUBEK

We can be seen from the hotel.

MAIA

We are still married—aren't we?
[No response.]
Fine.

[She sits.]
What is it that you want to say?

RUBEK
[After a long pause.]
Why was it, do you suppose, that I finally agreed to this little vacation?

MAIA
I don't know. Something about it being good for my spirits. At least, that's what you said. But—

RUBEK
But—?

MAIA
I don't believe that anymore.

RUBEK
What then.

MAIA
I think it was on account of the pale lady.

RUBEK
Madame von Satow?

MAIA
She's always hanging at our heels—watching. It's as if she's waiting for something terrible to happen—waiting for me to fall off a cliff or disappear in the mountains so she can take my place. And last night, she made her way up here as well—followed, of course, by that witch of hers.

RUBEK
[Feigning surprise.]
Did she?

MAIA
Oh, don't pretend. I know very well that you knew her long before you ever knew me.

RUBEK

And had forgotten her, too—long before I knew you.

MAIA

Can you forget so easily?

RUBEK

When I want to, yes.

MAIA

Even a woman who has modeled for you? One who has stood before you naked?

RUBEK

A true artist must move freely from one inspiration to the next. He mustn't allow himself to become entangled.

MAIA

Like you have?

RUBEK

What do you mean?

MAIA

With me.
[Long pause; staring at the ground.]
It was the pale lady that brought us here. I'm quite sure of it.

RUBEK

And how was I to know she had returned to the country?

MAIA

You saw her name in one of the papers.

RUBEK

But she's married now—I've never heard of any Herr von Satow.

MAIA

Her picture then.

RUBEK

No. You're on the wrong track. It was for another reason entirely, and that is what we must sooner or later have an honest discussion about.

[Pause.]

You said this morning that I have become very restless as of late. What do you think might be the reason for that?

MAIA

How should I know? Perhaps you've grown tired of me.

RUBEK

Perhaps.

MAIA

[Rising angrily.]

If you want to get rid of me, all you have to do is say so!

RUBEK

Sit down.

MAIA

I will not! If you want to have done with me, please say so right out, and I will go this instant!

RUBEK

Do you intend that as a threat, Maia?

MAIA

Yes!

[A short pause.]

No.

[She sits.]

There can be no threat for you in that.

[Pause.]

RUBEK

We cannot possibly go on living like this.

MAIA

No.

RUBEK

What has become so painfully clear these past few months, is that I require a . . . a confidante . . . someone to share all my victories and my defeats—

MAIA

Don't I do that?

RUBEK

Not in the sense that . . . what I need is the companionship of an . . . an equal, so to speak.

MAIA

An equal?

RUBEK

One who can . . . complete me . . . supply in me what is wanting . . . be one with me in all my striving.

MAIA

I can see that you have someone specific in mind.

RUBEK

You can see that, can you?

MAIA

I know you better than you think, Rubek.
[Pause.]
Do you know the people at the hotel think she's mad?

RUBEK

And what, pray tell, do the people at the hotel think of your bear-killer?
[Pause.]
I've grown quite fond of you, Maia. I have. And I don't want you to feel as if you've failed in any way. On the contrary, you've been a delightful companion. But I have found myself sinking, more and more, into long periods of darkness. And what I've come to realize is this: I am simply not suited for the leisurely pursuit of happiness. Life doesn't shape itself that way for me. I must go on working, you see—producing one work of art after another—right up until my dying day, or else I will simply waste away.

MAIA

What does that have to do with—

RUBEK

Madame von Satow?

MAIA

I was going to say with me.

RUBEK

[Pauses, laying a hand on his breast.]
In here, you see—in here I have a little lock-box . . . and in that box are stored up all my sculptor's visions . . . inspirations for all my future works. When she left, Madame von Satow, when she disappeared without a trace, the lock of that box snapped shut. She had the key, you see—she took it with her—so all of those visions, they were left unrealized. All of those treasures—wasted. The years pass, and I have no means of getting at them. I can only fumble at the lock.

MAIA

Didn't I inspire you at all, Rubek? Even a little bit?

RUBEK

You reminded me of her . . . of Irene, as she once was . . . years ago. You are more alike than you might suspect. That's what drew me to you. But you, little Maia . . . you had no key.
[Pause.]

MAIA

Then you must get her to open this box for you. You make such a fuss over the simplest things.

RUBEK

Do you really think it's that simple?

MAIA

Of course. You attach yourself to whomever you most require. It's nothing to be ashamed of, Professor. I'll manage. I can always run off to the villa, if necessary, but I don't think it will come to that. I'm sure in town—in that great big house of ours—surely there must be room enough for three.

RUBEK

For three?

MAIA

That's right.

RUBEK

You mean—

MAIA

I'm sure we can still be of some use to one another. And if it doesn't work out, well, we will simply get out of each other's way—part entirely. No need to be anxious about that.

RUBEK

You're taking this all rather well.

MAIA

I am, perhaps, more grown up than some people might think.

RUBEK

So it would seem.

[Pause.]

MAIA

Look! There she is—your key.

RUBEK

Where?

MAIA

There—coming out of the forest. Striding like a marble statue. She's coming this way.

RUBEK

She is the Resurrection incarnate—even after all these years.

[Pause.]

MAIA

Go. Talk to her.

RUBEK

What about you?

MAIA

The bear-killer awaits.

[She starts to go . . . hesitates.]

If you'd like, I'll bring you back a bird of prey to model. I'll shoot one for you.

[RUBEK nods. MAIA exits. After a moment, IRENE appears. She stares at RUBEK, but keeps her distance. Silence.]

RUBEK

You don't have your friend with you today.

IRENE

No.

[Hesitates.]

She is keeping an eye on me, none the less.

RUBEK

Is she?

IRENE

Wherever I may go. She never loses sight of me.

[Whispering.]

Until, one fine sunny morning, I shall kill her!

RUBEK

Kill her?

IRENE

With the utmost delight—if only I could manage it.

RUBEK

What's stopping you?

IRENE

She deals in witchcraft.

[Agitated.]

Arnold—she has changed herself into my shadow!

RUBEK

Well . . . we must all have a shadow, I suppose.

[Pause.]

IRENE

Why are you staring at me like that?

RUBEK

I . . . I still can't believe you've come back to me. After all these years.

IRENE

You think I'm insane.

RUBEK

No.

IRENE

I have come from the uttermost regions, **Arnold**. From the great dead waste. You cannot expect me to be what I was. I see **things** differently now. My eyes have been opened.

RUBEK

Tell me what you see.

IRENE

What?

RUBEK

With these new eyes of yours. Tell me, Irene. I want to understand you. I want to see the world as you see it.

IRENE

That isn't possible.

RUBEK

Why not?

IRENE

You . . . are not capable.

RUBEK

Describe it to me—this world of yours.

IRENE

There are no words.

RUBEK

Make new ones!

IRENE

You wouldn't understand, Arnold. You couldn't. You'd only misinterpret.

RUBEK

Let me try. Please? For old times' sake.
                    [Pause.]
Close your eyes.
                    [She does.]
Now . . . tell me what you see.

IRENE

Chaos.

RUBEK

Go on.

IRENE

No boundaries. Everything . . . overlapping . . . inverted . . . backwards. Fragments of life . . . racing by . . . little bits . . . pieces . . . skipping like stones . . . flashing briefly in the darkness.
                    [Pause.]
That's all there is. Fragments. Passing bits.

RUBEK

It's very poetic—this world of yours.
                    [Pause.]
I think I'll sculpt it.

IRENE

What? No!

RUBEK

Yes! This chaos! You will describe it to me, as best you can—every detail! And I will drag it unwillingly into the light! I will illuminate its darkest corners!

IRENE

Arnold!

RUBEK

e up my mind. I will understand these visions of yours, Irene. I will immerse myself in them. And, in so doing, I will find you again.

IRENE

I told you! I warned you—you wouldn't understand!

RUBEK

I don't pretend to understand yet, but—

IRENE

You are lost! Lost!

RUBEK

Then help me find myself! Help me find the artist I once was!

IRENE

How can I when I hated him—this artist?!

RUBEK

You cared for me once.

IRENE

Never! Never! I pray every night that you will lose your soul as I have lost mine!

RUBEK

[Warmly.]

That's not true.

IRENE

It is! How could I *not* hate you, when you so carelessly took a young girl and wore the soul out of her, drained her essence because you needed it for a work of art?! I hated you because you could stand there so unaffected—

RUBEK

Do you really believe—

IRENE

Because you were an artist and an artist only! An observer! Not a man! But that child . . . that child in the wet, living clay . . . that young life, I loved . . . as it rose up

---

72

out of that raw, shapeless mass . . . as it took shape, a vital human creature . . . our daughter . . . it is for the sake of the child that I have returned.

RUBEK

I don't understand. You . . . you want to—

IRENE

I want to see it. I want to see *her*.

RUBEK

You want to see the . . . ?
[IRENE nods.]
You are unaware, perhaps, that she is housed in a great museum halfway around the world.

IRENE

I will make a pilgrimage to the place where my soul and my child's soul lie buried.
[Silence.]

RUBEK
[Decisively.]
No.

IRENE

What?

RUBEK

No. I can't allow it. You must never see that sculpture again. Never. Do you hear? Finished—in marble which you always thought so cold—I forbid it.

IRENE

You *forbid it?*

RUBEK

Yes. Absolutely.

IRENE

I will find the child with or without your help. You cannot keep her from me.

RUBEK

Irene, you . . . you don't understand!
[Almost to himself.]
How could you when you left before it was completed?

IRENE

Before she was . . . . What do you mean? How could I have left unless the child had been—

RUBEK

She was not . . . what she afterwards became.
[Unseen by RUBEK, IRENE quietly unsheathes a dagger which she carries in her breast.]

IRENE

[With a menacing tone.]
Arnold—have you done some evil to our child?!

RUBEK

Not according to the critics.

IRENE

Tell me! What have you done?!
[As he turns to look at her, she drops the knife to her side so that he cannot see it.]

RUBEK

I will tell you . . . but you must promise to sit quietly and hear me out. You mustn't pass judgment until I've told you everything.

IRENE

I will listen as quietly as a mother can when she—

RUBEK

And you mustn't look at me. Not until I've finished . . . I don't think I could bear it.

IRENE

All right . . . but you mustn't look at me either. You must turn your back until you have finished.

RUBEK

Fair enough.

[He turns his back to her.]

IRENE
[Still facing him—holding the dagger.]

Speak quickly.

RUBEK
[With difficulty.]

When I first found you . . . I knew at once I would make use of you for my life's work. You were what I required in every respect. I was young then—with no knowledge of the world—and I thought that *The Resurrection* would be most beautifully rendered as an innocent young woman, not yet corrupted by life, awakening to light and glory without having to put away from her anything ugly or impure.

IRENE

Yes. And so I stand now—in our work.

RUBEK

Not entirely.

[Pause.]

You have said that I cannot expect you to be the same woman I knew all those years ago. Well, I am not the man I once was either, Irene. In the years that followed your departure, I became schooled in the ways of the world. My vision of "The Resurrection Day" evolved—became more . . . complex. Your solitary, unsullied figure no longer expressed my conception, and I . . . I made modifications.

IRENE

Do I not stand as I always stood for you?

RUBEK

Yes . . . yes, but . . . there are others.

IRENE

Others?

RUBEK

I looked at the world around me . . . and I had no choice but to include what I saw. Women and men as I knew them in real life.

IRENE

—with our child?! Strangers?!

RUBEK

At the base of the sculpture, I created fissures in the ground, and from this hell-mouth, there are now men and women with dimly-suggested animal faces, swarming up around the child, pulling her down as she tries to rise up into the heavens.

IRENE

My eternal soul . . . you and I . . . we . . . we and our child . . . we lived in that solitary figure!

RUBEK

Yes—we! *We!* I had to include myself, you see. I had to put a little bit of myself into the girl—that glorious figure who can't quite free herself from this earth—who reaches with her hands for the heavens, for perfection, tortured by the knowledge that she will never attain her goal, never escape, that she will remain forever imprisoned in this . . . this hell!

IRENE

[Raising the knife over RUBEK's head.]

Poet! You have killed my soul—the soul of our child—so you model yourself in remorse, and with that you think your account is cleared?!

RUBEK

[Oblivious.]

I am an artist, Irene. And try as I may, I shall never be anything else.

IRENE

Yes . . . you are an artist. But *I* was a human being! I had a life to live, Arnold—a human destiny to fulfill! And I let that slip away to become your . . . your slave! Your whore! It was suicide! An unforgivable sin against myself! A sin for which I can never atone! I should have borne children! Many children! Real children! Not clay creatures! Not such children as are hidden away in museums! That was my vocation! To bring life into this world! To be a mother!

[Pause.]

I ought never to have served you.

RUBEK

[Lost in his memories.]

And yet . . . those were beautiful days.

IRENE
[Looks at him strangely.]
What?

RUBEK
Beautiful, wondrous days. I would not trade them for anything.
[Pause. IRENE lowers the knife.]

IRENE
Do you remember what you said—the day you finished?

RUBEK
No. What did I say?

IRENE
[Astonished.]
You don't remember?

RUBEK
I . . . I'm sorry. My mind isn't what it used to be.

IRENE
You took my hands and pressed them to you. And I waited. I waited, Arnold.
Breathless. For what seemed like an eternity, I waited! And then you said to me,
"Thank you. Thank you, Irene. This has been a priceless episode."

RUBEK
Did I really say that? *Episode?*
[Pause.]
I'm sure I didn't mean—

IRENE
At that word, I left you.

RUBEK
You take everything so painfully to heart.

IRENE
And you take nothing.

RUBEK

That's not true.
[Pause.]
Do you recall the summer we spent on the Lake of Taunitz—every weekend?

IRENE

Yes. After our work was done.

RUBEK

We'd take the train out to the lake and sit beside that little peasant hut.

IRENE

It was an episode, Arnold.

RUBEK

You used to take water-lilies, I remember—you'd tell me they were birds and set them swimming in the brook.
[Pause.]

IRENE

Swans.

RUBEK

What?

IRENE

Swans. They were white swans.

RUBEK

Yes. Of course. How fond you were of that game! We played it the whole summer. I remember, once, I took a great furry leaf and fastened it to one of the swans—a burdock-leaf, I believe it was—and you said it was Lohengrin's boat, with the swan yoked to it. I said you were the swan that drew my boat.
[Pause.]
I bought that little hut—beside the Lake of Taunitz.

IRENE

Did you?

RUBEK

Yes.

———

IRENE

You often said you would. If you could afford it.
[Pause.]
And it still stands—the little hut?

RUBEK

No. I had it pulled down. I couldn't bear to see it standing there—it filled me with such sadness. In its place there is a magnificent villa.

IRENE

And you live there now—with the other one?

RUBEK

When we aren't traveling. Yes.
[Pause.]

IRENE

Life was beautiful by the Lake of Taunitz. But we let it slip away—that life and all its beauty.

RUBEK

You could come and live with us—in the villa.

IRENE

With the two of you?

RUBEK

With me. You can set your swans swimming in the brook . . . we can talk of old times . . . you can open all that is locked up in me—as you did in our days of creation.

IRENE

I no longer have the key to you, Arnold.

RUBEK

You do! You and no one else! I beg of you, Irene—give me this one chance to live my life over again. Help me undo my greatest mistake.

IRENE

There is no resurrection for the life we once led, you and I. Time moves forward only.

RUBEK
let us pretend! Let us pretend we are still on that lake! That we never left!

IRENE
It would only be an illusion.

RUBEK
I don't care! Better to live an illusion than to continue with this . . . this darkness! When you left, Irene . . . when you disappeared . . . I cannot express to you . . . I was filled with such regret. I became painfully aware of all that I had left unsaid . . . all the moments I had allowed to pass . . . without . . . without grasping them . . . without . . . I had come to think of you as something sacred, you see . . . something holy . . . a gift from God . . . a creature of innocence not to be touched save in adoring thoughts. A superstition took hold of me that if I touched you . . . if I desired you with my senses . . . my soul would be desecrated, and I would not be able to finish my work. I was a fool! An idealistic young fool! I should have taken you in my arms right then and there—on the floor of my studio, I should have taken you! With the clay still on my fingers! It would only have added to the beauty of the child—to the depth and complexity of her meaning—of her mystery.
[Pause.]
I can't lose you again, Irene—I don't think I could survive it.
[Pause.]

IRENE
Perhaps . . . we can arrange some sort of . . . compromise.

RUBEK
Compromise?

IRENE
Yes.

RUBEK
What do you mean?

IRENE
One night together. One last night. I can't promise anything more.

RUBEK
Yes! Yes! Do you really mean it?

IRENE

On one condition.

RUBEK

Anything!

IRENE

You must never sculpt again.

[RUBEK stares at her, dumbfounded.]

RUBEK

Never?

IRENE

You mustn't even speak of it.

[Pause.]

RUBEK

You . . . you want me to give up my life's work? Give it up entirely?

IRENE

It's a small price to pay—don't you think? For one night of real happiness. For the chance to relive your fondest memories.

RUBEK

Irene—

IRENE

[Suddenly agitated.]

Wait!

RUBEK

What?

IRENE

Shhh!

RUBEK

What is it?

IRENE

[He does.]

RUBEK

I don't—

IRENE

Don't look! She's watching us!

RUBEK

Who?

IRENE

The witch!

RUBEK

Your Sister of—

IRENE

I have to go.

RUBEK

Wait—

IRENE

Don't stand! She mustn't know our plans. Stay here. Don't follow me. I will come tonight. I will wait for you here. If you are willing to make this sacrifice . . .
[She pauses—stares at him for a long moment—touches his face.]
It's strange. What might have been. We see it only when . . .

RUBEK

When what?

IRENE

When we dead awaken . . . we see that we have never lived.
[She exits. RUBEK stares after her.]

*   *   *

ACT III

[A mountain-side. Enter MAIA, flushed and irritated. ULFHEIM follows—half angry, half laughing—clutching her by the sleeve.]

MAIA

Let me go! Let go!

ULFHEIM

What—are you going to bite now?

MAIA

Maybe!

ULFHEIM

Mmmm! Just like a she-wolf!

MAIA

Let go, I said!

[ULFHEIM laughs.]

That's it! I'm not going one more step with you! Not one more step—do you hear?!

ULFHEIM

Oh, no? And just how do you propose to get away from me—here on this mountain-side?

MAIA

I'll jump off that cliff, if necessary!

ULFHEIM

And mangle that pretty little body of yours? What a waste that would be!

MAIA

You're a fine one to go hunting with!

ULFHEIM

Sporting, let's say.

MAIA

Oh! So you call this sport—do you?

ULFHEIM

The kind of sport I like best of all.

MAIA

I thought you preferred bears.

ULFHEIM

Depends on my mood.
                    [Again, he grabs her—she pushes him away.]

MAIA

Why did you turn the dogs loose up there?

ULFHEIM

What?

MAIA

The dogs—why did you turn them loose?

ULFHEIM

What does it matter?

MAIA

Tell me!

ULFHEIM

So they might do a little hunting of their own.

MAIA

Liar! You let them go because you wanted to get rid of Lars!

ULFHEIM

Why would I want to do that?

MAIA

So you could molest me up here on the mountain-side!

ULFHEIM

Not a bad idea.

MAIA

If you touch me, I'll scream.

ULFHEIM

And bring the whole mountain down on top of us?

MAIA

Better to die in an avalanche than be groped by the likes of you!

ULFHEIM

Oh, it's not as bad as all that. I might even teach you a few things.

MAIA

Do you know what you are, Mr. Ulfheim? A faun! A wood-demon!

ULFHEIM

What is that—some sort of monster?

MAIA

Just the sort of creature you are! A hairy, smelly, bloated, ugly thing with a goat's beard and goat-legs, and horns, too!

ULFHEIM

Horns, did you say?

MAIA

That's right! A pair of ugly horns—just like yours!

ULFHEIM

Would you like to see my poor little horns, Maia?

MAIA

I can see them quite plainly, thank you.

ULFHEIM

Then I suppose I'd better see about tying you up.

MAIA

What?!

ULFHEIM

That's right.
                    [Taking a dog's leash out of his pocket.]
If I'm a demon, let me be a demon.

MAIA

You wouldn't dare!

ULFHEIM

Wouldn't I?
                    [Circling her.]
Have you ever been tied before, Maia?

MAIA

I should think not!

ULFHEIM

No? The Professor never strapped you to his desk for a little change-of-pace?
Laced your arms together behind your back?

MAIA

Mr. Ulfheim, please put that rope away.
                    [He continues to circle her.]
What would Lars think, if he were to return with the dogs?

ULFHEIM

Oh, there's no danger of that. Lars—he knows my . . . my methods of sport, you
see.

MAIA

Oh!

ULFHEIM

Now, are you going to play nice—or shall I lash you to this tree?

MAIA

This isn't fair, Mr. Ulfheim. You lured me here under false pretenses. You promised a magnificent hunting-castle.

ULFHEIM

There it is—right behind you.

MAIA

That old pig-stye?!

ULFHEIM

It serves its purpose. Two hunting companions can pass a summer's night in there comfortably enough. Or a whole summer, if it comes to that.

MAIA

Oh, you're no better than him!

ULFHEIM

Who—the Professor?

MAIA

Yes! The Professor! The village boys, before him! You're all alike! Every one of you! You'll promise anything to get what you want!

ULFHEIM

And what is it that we want?

MAIA

Do I really have to say it?
[She shrugs, resigned to her fate.]
Fine. Fine. If it means so much to you—just take it. Tie me to the tree and get it over with.

ULFHEIM
[Taken aback.]

What?

MAIA

You heard me.

[Pause. ULFHEIM hesitates.]

Well . . . go on.

[Pause.]

ULFHEIM

Let me tell you a story.

[MAIA laughs.]

What's so funny?

MAIA

You're going to tell me a story now?

ULFHEIM

Why not?

MAIA

Is it a dirty story, Mr. Ulfheim—something to get me in the mood?

ULFHEIM

Oh, no—this is a comical story.

MAIA

A comical one?

ULFHEIM

That's right.

MAIA

[Shrugs.]

Whatever turns you on.

ULFHEIM

Once upon a time, in a land very much like this one, there lived a young bear-hunter.

MAIA

A bear-hunter?

ULFHEIM

That's right.

MAIA

Is he the hero or the villain of the story—this bear hunter?

ULFHEIM

The hero, of course. He wasn't much to look at as heroes go, but he was happy, you see, for he was madly in love with a beautiful young girl. And she was in love with him, or so he thought. He took her—lifted her up from the filth and muck of the street—carried her in his arms. Next to his heart he carried her. And so he would have borne her all through life, lest she dash her foot against a stone—for her shoes were worn very thin when he found her.

MAIA

And yet he took her up and carried her next to his heart? How noble!

ULFHEIM

Make fun if you like, but he pulled her out of the gutter and carried her as high and as carefully as he could. He would have done anything for this girl. Anything! And do you know what he got for his pains?

MAIA

No. What did he get?

ULFHEIM

The horns! The horns that you now see so plainly! She left him for another as soon as she could manage it. An educated man—with better prospects. Is that not a comical story, madam bear-murderess?

MAIA

Oh yes, comical enough. But I know another story, more comical still.

ULFHEIM

Oh? And how does that story go?

MAIA

There once was a stupid young girl. Like your bear-hunter, she was happy enough. She had both a father and a mother. And a pleasant little home. But she was never quite satisfied, for this home was rather poor, you see, and she had a strange yearning for something more.

ULFHEIM

A common enough story.

MAIA

One day, a famous artist appeared in the little village, and he took the girl in his arms—as you did—and carried her far, far away from her pleasant little home.

ULFHEIM

Did she go willingly?

MAIA

Quite willingly—for she was stupid, you see.

ULFHEIM

And no doubt he was a handsome young artist.

MAIA

Not so handsome—or young, either. But he was clever, and he knew just what to say. He promised to take her to the top of the highest mountain, where she would live forever in the fresh air and sunshine.

ULFHEIM

He was a mountaineer as well?

MAIA

In his way.

ULFHEIM

And did he make good on his promise? Did he take the girl up with him?

MAIA

He *took* her, to be sure! Bewitched her with his fine talk and dropped her into a cold, clammy cage, where there was neither sunlight nor fresh air, but only death and great petrified ghosts of people skewered to the walls.

ULFHEIM

Serves her right!

MAIA

Do you really think so?

ULFHEIM

I do. She was only using this artist—just as he was using her.
[Pause. MAIA considers this.]

MAIA

I suppose you're right. Still, it's a comical story all the same.
[Pause.]
Did you know him?

ULFHEIM

What?

MAIA

The man she left you for—did you know him?

ULFHEIM

I met him once or twice.

MAIA

Did you hate him very much?

ULFHEIM

I hated them both.

MAIA

And didn't you want to take revenge on them somehow? Hurt them—like they had hurt you?

ULFHEIM

I did. For a long time. Yes. I thought about it every day.

MAIA

But you never actually *did* anything about it?

ULFHEIM

Oh, I played a nasty little trick on her once. Broke her spirit. Made both of them very unhappy for a long time.

MAIA

What sort of trick?

ULFHEIM

I'd rather not talk about it.

MAIA

Then . . . it didn't make you feel any better?

ULFHEIM

No. It did not.

[Pause.]

MAIA

Are you still going to tie me to that tree?

ULFHEIM

No, dammit. I don't have the heart for it, after all.

MAIA

Why, Mr. Ulfheim—you're turning out to be quite the gentleman.

ULFHEIM

Pah!

[Thunder. ULFHEIM peers into the distance.]

Storm's moving in.

MAIA

Is it going to rain?

ULFHEIM

It's going to do a lot more than that.

MAIA

I love the rain. I love to stand in it. It makes me feel . . . clean.

ULFHEIM

We'll have to start down.

MAIA

You don't want to stand in the rain with me, Mr. Ulfheim—be washed clean together?

ULFHEIM

There's not enough rain in the sky.

MAIA

What?

ULFHEIM

Nothing. We have to go. There isn't much time.

MAIA

[Laughs.]
You're not afraid of a little storm—are you?

ULFHEIM

You don't want to be caught up here, believe me.

MAIA

Are you serious?

ULFHEIM

Deadly serious.

MAIA

We're . . . we're not in any danger—are we?

ULFHEIM

I'm afraid so.

MAIA

From a little storm?

ULFHEIM

Not so little.

MAIA

What about Lars and the dogs?

ULFHEIM

They'll find their way. We'll have to take a different route down. It's a little more difficult.

MAIA

All right. Which way do we go?

ULFHEIM

Right down the face of that cliff.

MAIA

What?! Have you lost your mind?!

ULFHEIM

It's the quickest way down. I'll carry you on my back.

[MAIA goes to the edge of the precipice—peers down.]

MAIA

I . . . I couldn't possibly!

ULFHEIM

If we stay here, that storm will blow us right off the mountain.

MAIA

Why can't we go back the way we came?!

ULFHEIM

There isn't time.

MAIA

What about your cabin?! We could wait out the storm inside!

ULFHEIM

Might work. Of course, if the thunder causes an avalanche, we'd be buried alive.

[Thunder—louder this time.]

MAIA

Oh! How could I be so stupid?! I should have known better than to come tramping up here! The Professor was right—I wasn't made to be a mountain-climber!

ULFHEIM

[Peering over the cliff.]

I'll be damned!

MAIA

What?

ULFHEIM

There he is now!

MAIA

Who?

ULFHEIM

The Professor. And a woman, looks like.

MAIA

No! No, no, no! Can we get past them—without being seen?

ULFHEIM

You're not ashamed to be seen with an ugly, old bear-hunter—are you?

MAIA

It's not that. I . . . I don't want him to see me like this . . . helpless . . . clinging to your back like a frightened child. That's how he thinks of me, you know—like a little child that must always be watched after and reprimanded and talked down to.

ULFHEIM

I'm sorry, Maia. There's no other way.
            [Pause.]

MAIA

Fine then. We'll face them here.

ULFHEIM

That's the spirit.
            [After a moment, RUBEK and IRENE appear over the edge of the precipice.]

RUBEK

Maia! Well, what do you know!

MAIA
            [Coolly.]
Professor.

RUBEK

Mr. Ulfheim.

ULFHEIM

I'm surprised to find you at such a high altitude.

RUBEK

I used to do a bit of climbing in my younger days.

ULFHEIM

Did you come up that way there?

RUBEK

We did.

ULFHEIM

It's a dangerous path you've chosen.

RUBEK

It didn't seem particularly difficult at first.

ULFHEIM

Never does.

RUBEK

By the by, however, I must admit, we found that while it was increasingly difficult to move forward, it was quite impossible to go back.

ULFHEIM

The treachery of the mountains. She welcomes your company, but when you try to desert her—she can be damn temperamental.

IRENE
[Staring excitedly at ULFHEIM.]

I . . . I know you!
[Pause.]
Don't I? Don't I know you?

ULFHEIM
[Evasively.]

No.

IRENE

No? Are you sure?

[She touches his face.]

You remind me of a boy I once knew.

ULFHEIM

You must be mistaken.

IRENE

In another lifetime . . . or a dream, perhaps.

RUBEK

[Pulling IRENE's hand away from ULFHEIM's face.]

Irene . . . you're frightening Mr. Ulfheim.

IRENE

He reminds me of a boy . . .

[Thunder—louder now.]

ULFHEIM

Storm-blasts from the peaks!

RUBEK

It sounds like a prelude to the Resurrection Day!

ULFHEIM

Just look at those clouds! They'll soon be upon us—like a winding-sheet!

IRENE

[With a shiver.]

I know that sheet!

MAIA

[To RUBEK.]

It isn't safe here.

RUBEK

What?

MAIA

It isn't safe.

ULFHEIM

She's right.

RUBEK

What should we—

ULFHEIM

I can't help all of you. Take shelter in that cabin there—when the storm passes, I'll send someone to fetch the two of you away.

IRENE
[In terror.]

Fetch us away?!

ULFHEIM

As soon as possible. For your sake, pray that it passes quickly.

RUBEK

Surely it's not as bad as all that.

ULFHEIM

If you don't take Nature seriously, she will strike you down, Professor. She doesn't like to be trifled with. Come, Maia—grab hold of your wood-demon and hold on for dear life!

> *[MAIA goes to RUBEK and kisses him impulsively on the cheek.]*

MAIA

Goodbye, Professor.

> *[She climbs onto ULFHEIM's back. As they approach the precipice, MAIA covers her eyes.]*

MAIA

I can't look!

ULFHEIM

Maia—don't you dare close your eyes!

> *[MAIA and ULFHEIM disappear over the side of the cliff.]*

IRENE

Did you hear, Arnold?! Did you hear?! Men are coming to fetch me away! She will come too! She must have missed me by now! Oh, Arnold—she'll be angry! She'll put me in the straitjacket! She has it with her! In her box! I've seen it with my own eyes!

RUBEK

No one will to touch you, Irene. No one. I won't allow it.

IRENE

She's watching us—even now! With those eyes! Those dark eyes! She's put a curse on us, Arnold—I'm sure of it! A curse for our sins against Nature!

RUBEK

There is no one here, Irene—only us.
                    [He holds her.]
Only us.
                    [Pause.]

IRENE

Still . . . if she comes—

RUBEK

If she comes, I will pitch her over the precipice! Right into the abyss!

IRENE
                [Staring at him coldly.]
You're mocking me now.

RUBEK

No—

IRENE

You don't believe a word I've said! You think it's only the . . . the ravings of a madwoman!

RUBEK

Irene—

IRENE

She will come, Arnold—you will see! She will reveal her true self! But this time—this time, I'm prepared for her! I won't return to the grave without a fight! I will defend myself! I have a weapon!

RUBEK

A weapon?

IRENE

[Drawing the knife.]
Yes! Always! Always! Both day and night!

RUBEK

Give me the knife.

IRENE

No! You would leave me defenseless!

RUBEK

Irene . . . listen to me . . . what use can you have for it here?

IRENE

What use?

RUBEK

No one can reach you here—on this mountain. Surely you can see that.

IRENE

She is coming!

RUBEK

She's only a Sister of Mercy—sent to watch over you.

IRENE

No!

RUBEK

Do you really believe . . . do you think she can *transport* herself through the storm and—

IRENE

She knows no boundaries, Arnold!

RUBEK

Then what use is a knife—against such a powerful foe?

IRENE

It wasn't meant for her.

RUBEK

What?

IRENE

It . . . it wasn't meant for her. The knife.
                    [Pause.]
It was meant for *you.*

RUBEK

For me?

IRENE

Yes.

RUBEK

But . . . why would you—

IRENE

Last night . . . as we were sitting by the Lake of Taunitz—

RUBEK

By the Lake of—

IRENE

—outside the little peasant's hut . . . playing with swans . . . when I heard you say with such icy coldness that I had been nothing more than an episode in your life—

RUBEK

You said it, Irene, not—

IRENE

—I felt for the knife . . . I had it in my hand. I wanted to stab you with it. I would have.

RUBEK

But you didn't.

IRENE

No.

RUBEK

Why not?

IRENE

Because I suddenly realized . . . it came to me in a flash . . . that you were already dead. You and I both, Arnold. Long ago. So we sat there by the Lake of Taunitz—two cold, clay bodies—and comforted one another.

RUBEK

I don't call that being dead.

IRENE

No? Then where is the burning desire you felt for me once—all those years ago—that you claim to have battled so fiercely when I posed for you?

RUBEK

Perhaps you should pose for me now—as you did then—and see if I can't summon that same desire.

IRENE

No. I . . . it wouldn't be the same.

RUBEK

Why not?

IRENE

You don't know who I am—what I've become.

RUBEK

I know you, Irene.

IRENE

No—

RUBEK

I know you.

IRENE

I have stood on turn-tables naked.

RUBEK

I don't care.

IRENE

I have exposed myself to thousands of men after you. Performed acts for them.

RUBEK

I drove you to it. I was blind.

IRENE

Stop—

RUBEK

I placed a dead clay-image above the happiness of life—of love.

IRENE

Stop it! Why are you . . . why are you saying these things now?! Now, when it's too late!

RUBEK

There is still time, Irene—time to live our lives! If we are dead, then let two of the dead rise up, for once, and live life to the fullest—drink from the cup of happiness before we go to our graves! Let us mingle these two cold, clay bodies! Let us feel the warmth of real joy!

IRENE

Yes! Yes!

RUBEK

But not here. Not here in the half darkness—with this dark cloud hovering over us.

IRENE

No, no—up in the light! In the sunshine!

RUBEK

Yes! On the mountain-top! There we will hold our marriage-feast, Irene.

IRENE

The sun will warm us, Arnold. It will thaw our frigid bones.

RUBEK

All the powers of light will witness our union. We will live out our lives together—hand in hand. We will climb mountains—sleep under the stars. And we will have children. Many beautiful children!

IRENE

Children?

RUBEK

Yes!

IRENE

But . . . I'm . . . I'm too old—

RUBEK

Not children of that sort.

IRENE

Arnold . . . no. You promised.

RUBEK

It will be different this time, Irene! You'll see! We will make children of love and happiness! Not cold, infertile, soulless things, but creatures of light and joy! Boys and girls—dancing, singing, laughing! Bursting with life! We will make such beautiful children!

IRENE

And what of our firstborn? Have you forgotten her?

RUBEK

That first was no child! It was a miscarriage! An abomination! We tried to create life in a vacuum! That was our mistake! How could we breathe life into the child when we had no life of our own? But now . . . Irene, I am wide awake for the first time! You have opened my eyes as if from a dream! You say you were meant to be a mother—that that was your destiny—to have many children. Then help me spread this happiness that I feel with you. Be my muse. We will fashion children of great beauty in marble and clay and send them out into the world. We will people the earth with light and goodness!

IRENE

Oh, if only that were true!

RUBEK

It is! It is true!

IRENE

No . . . even now, we are only pretending.

RUBEK

Irene—?

IRENE

We still sit beside the Lake of Taunitz . . . not quite touching. Even now.
[Thunder. Lightning.]

RUBEK

If only I could . . . I don't know how to pull you from this darkness.

IRENE

I have been too long gone. In the grave, I mean.

RUBEK

Why do you cling to this delusion of death? Don't you see, it's only a . . . a coping mechanism of some sort . . . a trick of the mind to help you deal with certain—

IRENE

I expected too much of you.

RUBEK

What?

IRENE

You're not capable of making the sacrifice—I see that now.

RUBEK

But I—

IRENE

I am only a means to an end. Fuel for your real passion.

RUBEK

That's not true!

IRENE

It *is* true, Arnold. It has always been true.

RUBEK

No! No! I would do anything for you!

IRENE

You cannot comprehend the words you are speaking. They are meaningless repetitions of words you have heard others speak—others who were actually living.

RUBEK

Please . . . Irene . . . don't . . . it was only a momentary weakness.

IRENE

One that will return again and again.

RUBEK

No! Without you, my work is meaningless! It's nothing to me! I . . . I only want to make you happy! We won't talk of it again!

IRENE

You don't have the strength. There is only one thing that can separate you from your art, one thing—and that is death. Only then will you be mine. Only then will you look at me without distraction. Are you willing to make that sacrifice? Will you descend into darkness for me, Arnold? Will you follow me to the grave?

RUBEK

I will follow you anywhere!

IRENE

Anywhere?

RUBEK

Anywhere!

IRENE

[Holds out her hand.]
Then come—be my bridegroom here on this mountain-top?

RUBEK

Yes! Yes!
[He kisses her.]
Oh, Irene . . . I will be faithful! So faithful! I won't even speak of the other! Never again! Not even in a moment of weakness! You'll see! I'll show you!

IRENE

We must climb higher—through the mist—

RUBEK

Yes, through the mist—and through the storm—and then right up to the summit in all its glory! We have so much lost time to make up for! So much—
[Suddenly a sound like thunder is heard high above, followed by a loud rumbling.]
What's that?
[The rumbling continues, grows louder, gains momentum.]
What's happening? Is it—

IRENE

It is our wedding song.
[IRENE takes RUBEK'S hand as he looks around in confusion. Suddenly the stage goes dark. The rumbling crescendos—then fades to nothing. After a few moments, the SISTER OF MERCY emerges from the darkness. She stands silent for a moment, then removes her hood—it is IRENE. She makes the sign of the cross before her in the air. Slow fade to black.]

*　　*　　*

107

Breinigsville, PA USA
15 September 2009
224080BV00001B/40/P